THE USBORNE BOOK OF
EASY
PIANO
DUETS

Caroline Hooper

Designed by Joanne Pedley

Illustrated by Simone Abel

Original music and arrangements by Caroline Hooper

Series editor: Anthony Marks

About this book

Duets are tunes for two players. The duets in this book are for two people to play on one piano. At first the tunes are fairly easy, but they get harder as you go through the book. On some of the pages, you will find tips on how to play the pieces. Signs and symbols that may be unfamiliar to you are explained as they appear in the music.

Where to sit

To play the tunes in this book, the two players have to sit side by side at the piano. If you are sitting on the left-hand side, you play the music on the left-hand page, called Part B. If you are sitting on the right-hand side, you play the music on the right-hand page (Part A).

To a wild rose (Part B)

This tune is by Edward MacDowell, an American composer. Play it very smoothly. *Adagio* means "slowly".

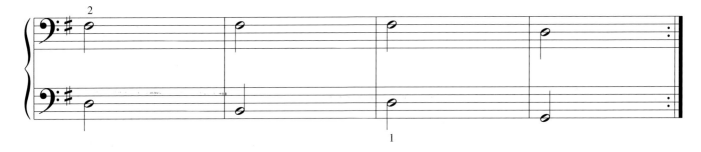

2

Before you play

Always look carefully at the music before you start to play. Find out how many beats there are in each measure, and see if there are any sharps or flats. Sometimes Part A may have two treble clefs and Part B may have two bass clefs. Check this before you begin.

Starting to play

It might help if you each practice your own part before playing together. Both players need to start at exactly the same time. To help you to do this, count a measure together before you start.

To *a wild rose* (Part A)

There is a sign in the tune below called a repeat. It tells you to go back to the beginning and play the tune again.

Keep going!

When you are playing duets, try to keep going all the way to the end of the piece, even if one player makes a mistake.

The merry-go-round

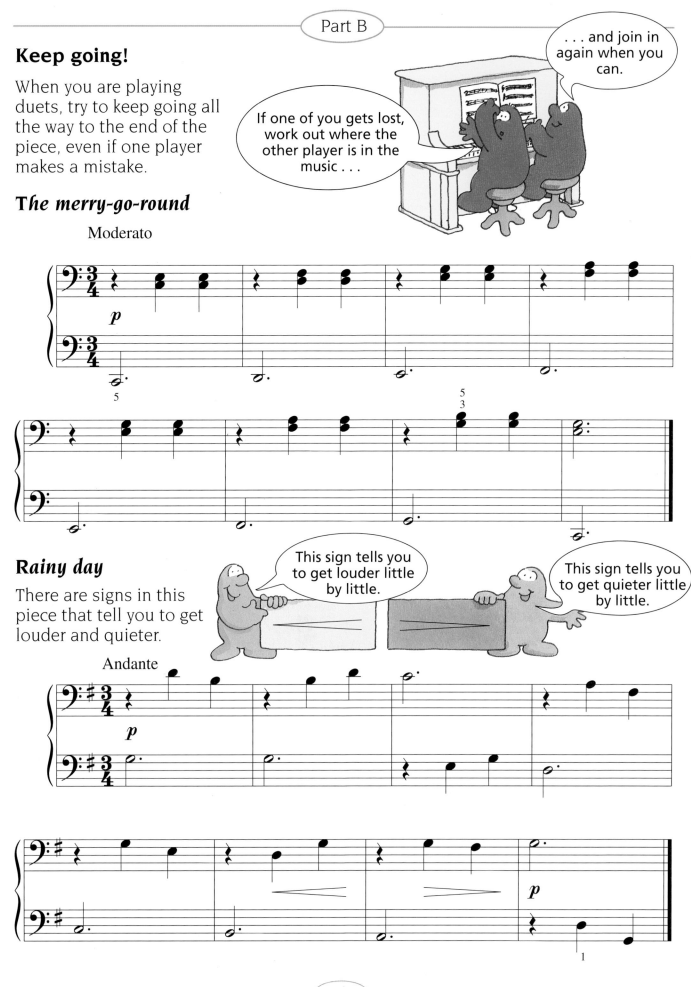

Moderato

Rainy day

There are signs in this piece that tell you to get louder and quieter.

Andante

Counting

When you are playing duets, it is important to keep an even beat throughout the piece. Try counting silently to yourself as you play.

The merry-go-round

> The letter *p* tells you to play quietly.

> *Moderato* means "play at a moderate speed". Don't play too quickly . . .

> . . . and don't play too slowly.

Rainy day

Andante means "at a walking pace", a little slower than *Moderato*.

> Make sure you count carefully.

> Watch out for the rests.

5

Playing tips

If you find playing together difficult, first make sure you each know your own part. Then play the piece together, in sections. When you can play each section without any mistakes, go back to the beginning and play the whole piece.

Lullaby

This tune is by a composer called Johannes Brahms.

Adagio

Grace notes

The next tune contains small notes called grace notes. Grace notes are used to decorate the music and make it more interesting. Play them very quickly, just before the main beat. Be careful to keep playing in time.

Lullaby

Play this tune very quietly and smoothly.

Different endings

Some tunes have two endings called first- and second-time measures.

Skaters' waltz

Allegretto means "fairly fast, but not too fast".

Musette

This tune was written by a German composer called Johann Sebastian Bach.

Tied notes

Sometimes two notes on the same line or space are joined, or tied, together.

Skaters' waltz

Remember to count the tied notes very carefully.

Musette

A musette is a type of dance which was popular in the 18th century.

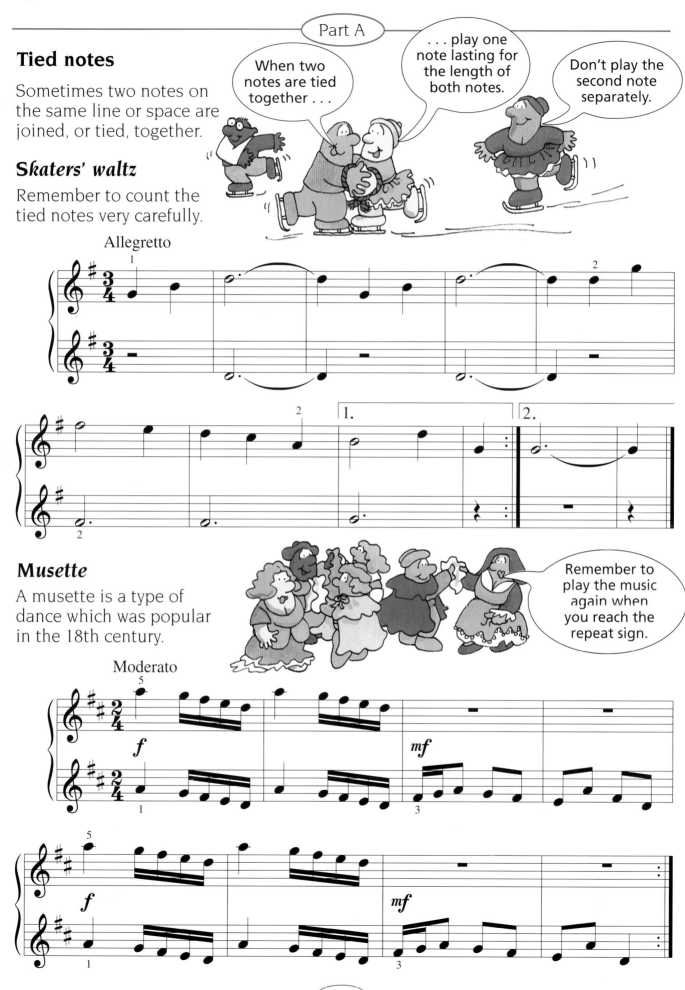

Surprise symphony

This piece is by Joseph Haydn, an Austrian composer. A symphony is a long piece of music in several different sections. It is played by a large group of instruments called an orchestra.

Look out for the letters telling you how loud to play. Try to make a difference between the loud and quiet parts.

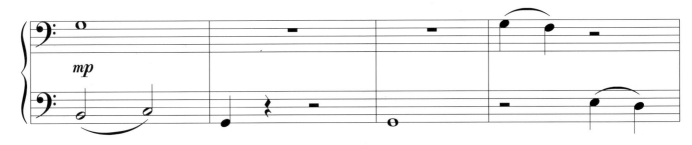

Surprise symphony

Ledger lines

Notes are written on ledger lines when they are too high or too low to be written on the staff.

This note is the first F above middle C.

This note is the third G below middle C.

The jolly peasant

Slumber song

Play the eighth notes very evenly, and try not to rush them. Look out for the rests.

Lento means "very slowly".

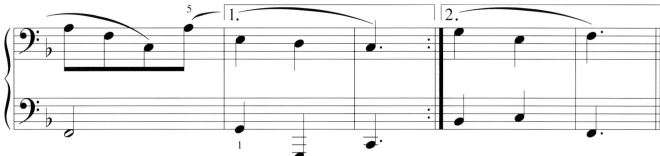

Working out the notes

To work out which notes to play, you can count up or down from the last note on the staff.

The jolly peasant

Slumber song

Legato means "smoothly". Remember to play quietly all the way through.

Playing tips

Don't start off too quickly. The first time through, always play at a speed you can manage. When you can both play the piece without any mistakes, try playing it a little faster.

German dance

This tune is by Wolfgang Amadeus Mozart, an Austrian composer.

D.C. al Fine

D.C. *al Fine* stands for *Da Capo al Fine*. This tells you to go back to the beginning of the piece and play the music again until you reach the word *Fine*. Then stop playing.

German dance

German dances were very popular all over Europe during the 18th century.

Playing tips

Always check the clefs at the beginning of the music. In the tune below, the right-hand part is in the treble clef.

Jumping beans

Allegro means "fast."

Try to make a difference between the loud and quiet sections.

Allegro

In the hall of the mountain king

The dots above and below the notes tell you to play these notes *staccato*.

Staccato means "short and spiky".

Alla marcia means "like a march".

Alla Marcia

Playing higher

Sometimes you have to play part of the music higher than it is written. The sign *8va* tells you to do this.

Jumping beans

In the hall of the mountain king

This tune was written by a Norwegian composer called Edvard Grieg.

17

Playing tips

Play the first beat of each measure a little louder than the others. This will help you to count more easily.

Hungarian dance no.5

This tune was written by Johannes Brahms, a German composer. Brahms was a very good pianist, and he wrote many pieces of music for the piano.

Playing smoothly

Play Part A very smoothly, so there is a big difference between this and the *staccato* notes in Part B.

Hungarian dance no.5

Brahms was very interested in music from different countries. He wrote four books of dances in the style of Hungarian music. This is one of them.

You have to play loudly throughout the piece.

Rainbow rag

This tune is in a style known as ragtime, an early form of jazz. Ragtime was very popular at the beginning of this century.

Remember to check the clefs at the beginning of the music.

Andante

Stealin' away

This tune is based on a Brazilian dance rhythm called a bossa nova. Make sure you count the tied notes very carefully.

Bossa nova players often use tambourines, maracas and other rhythm instruments.

Moderato

Rainbow rag

The rhythm in Part A of this tune is fairly tricky. Before playing the whole piece on the piano, try clapping the rhythm on its own first.

Stealin' away

Watch out for the rhythm in this tune. It will help if you each learn your own part before playing the music together.

Musical terms

There are two new musical terms in the tune below. *Dolce* means "sweet", so play the music very gently and quietly. *Andantino* means "a little faster than Andante".

Prelude in A

This tune was written by a Polish composer called Fryderyk Chopin. He was a very famous pianist.

Pause marks

A pause mark over a note tells you to make it last a little bit longer than usual. There is a pause mark in the tune below, at the end of the third line.

Prelude in A

A prelude is a short piece of music. Chopin wrote lots of piano music, including twenty-four preludes.

Lazy day

Play this tune very smoothly and slowly. Watch out for the signs telling you when to play loudly and quietly.

Adagio

Mazurka

This tune is by a French composer called Léo Delibes. It is from a ballet called Coppélia. A ballet is a dance set to music.

Allegretto

Lazy day

In the right-hand of Part A, make sure you start playing on the second B flat above middle C.

Mazurka

A mazurka is a country dance from Poland. It was very popular in France and Germany during the 18th century, and later in Britain.

D.S. al Fine

D.S. *al Fine* stands for *Dal Segno al Fine*. This means you play part of the music again.

Pizzicato polka

Allegro

Playing tips

When the notes are marked *staccato*, take your fingers off the keys very quickly.

Pizzicato polka

Venetian boat song no.1

This tune was written by a German composer called Felix Mendelssohn. Watch out for the pause marks.

Venetian boat song no.1

Sostenuto means sustained, so make sure you hold each note for its full time value and play very smoothly.

Andante sostenuto

Playing tips

Try to play the chords in Part B very gently. If they are too heavy, you might not be able to hear the tune in Part A.

An die Musik

The title of this tune means "To music". It was written by an Austrian composer called Franz Schubert.

Cantabile means "in a singing style".

Don't rush the eighth notes.

Playing together

The eighth notes in the right-hand of Part B and the left-hand of Part A must be played at exactly the same time.

An die Musik

Schubert wrote lots of music for the piano and other instruments, as well as more than six hundred songs. This is one of them.

This note is the third E above middle C.

Moderato

p   *cantabile*

Playing tips

It can be easier to play duets if you know what each part sounds like, so try to learn both parts of each duet before you play them with a friend.

If you know both parts, you can also have fun changing from one to the other.

One day you could play Part A.

The next day you could play Part B.

If you don't have someone else to play duets with, you could record yourself playing one part, then join in with the tape. To do this, count a bar or two out loud on the tape before you start playing. This will help you to know when to start playing the second part.

Index of tunes

First published in 1995 by Usborne Publishing Ltd., Usborne House, 83-85 Saffron Hill, London EC1N 8RT, England.

Printed in Portugal.